Boss of the World

by Fran Manushkin

illustrated by Tammie Lyon

Picture Window Books
Minneapolis, Minnesota

Katie Woo is published by Picture Window Books
A Capstone Imprint
1710 Roe Crest Drive
North Mankato, MN 56003
www.capstonepub.com

Library of Congress Cataloging-in-Publication Data
Manushkin, Fran.
  Boss of the world / by Fran Manushkin; illustrated by Tammie Lyon.
  p. cm. — (Katie Woo)
  ISBN 978-1-4048-5493-2 (library binding)
  ISBN 978-1-4048-6058-2 (softcover)
  ISBN 978-1-4795-2094-7 (e-book)
  [1. Bossiness—Fiction. 2. Behavior—Fiction. 3. Beaches—Fiction.
4. Chinese Americans—Fiction.] I. Lyon, Tammie, ill. II. Title.

  PZ7.M3195Bo 2010

  [E]—dc22   2009001860

Summary: When Katie Woo and her friends go to the beach, Katie is so rude and bossy that her friends do not want to play with her.

Creative Director: Heather Kindseth
Graphic Designer: Emily Harris

Photo Credits
  Fran Manushkin, pg. 26
  Tammie Lyon, pg. 26

Printed in the United States of America
in North Mankato, MN.
072015   009072R

Table of Contents

Chapter 1
Katie Acts Bossy 5

Chapter 2
Swings and Shells 11

Chapter 3
No More Meanie 18

Chapter 1
Katie Acts Bossy

Katie Woo and her friends

took a trip to the beach.

"Let's do everything

together!" said Katie. "We'll

have so much fun!"

"Let's build the biggest sand castle in the world!" shouted Pedro.

"You two carry the water
to me. I will build the castle,"
said Katie.

"That's not fun!" JoJo said.

"I think it is," replied Katie.

When the castle was finished, it wasn't very big, and it kept falling down.

"What a rotten castle!" Katie moaned.

At lunchtime, Katie shouted, "I'm so hungry, I could eat an elephant!"

"Me too!" said JoJo and Pedro.

They passed French fries around, but Katie ate most of them.

JoJo and Pedro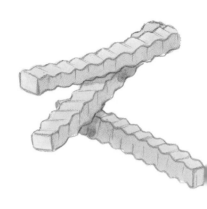

had only three

fries each.

"I'm still hungry," said

Pedro.

Katie grinned. "I'm not!"

she said.

Chapter 2
Swings and Shells

After lunch, Katie said,

"Let's lie on the blanket. We

can watch the clouds and

kites flying by."

"Katie, move over!" Pedro said. "You are taking up all of the blanket!"

"It's my blanket," Katie said. She did not move one inch. Pedro and JoJo had to lie on the itchy sand.

"Let's go over to the playground," Pedro said. "There are big swings there."

The three friends raced each other. Katie got there first and grabbed the only empty swing.

JoJo and Pedro watched
her swinging for a while.
Then they walked away.

"What's wrong with
them?" Katie wondered.

She ran after

her friends,

saying, "Let's

look for seashells!"

The three friends took

off their shoes. They walked

barefoot along the shore.

The waves tickled their toes.

"I see a giant shell!"

Pedro shouted.

He began running. But he
tripped over some driftwood
and fell down.

Katie grabbed the seashell.

"Hey, that's not fair!"
said JoJo. "Pedro saw the
giant shell first."

"Finders keepers," Katie
insisted.

JoJo and Pedro made
faces and walked away.

Chapter 3
No More Meanie

Katie grabbed her beach

ball and began tossing it

around, but it wasn't any fun.

Just then, JoJo and Pedro and JoJo's dad began swimming and splashing around in the waves.

Katie ran over, shouting,

"I want to swim too!"

"No!" yelled JoJo. "You

can't! The sea belongs to us!"

"That's silly," Katie said.

She laughed. "The sea can't

belong to you."

"And all the French
fries don't belong to you,"
said Pedro.

"And all the seashells,"
added JoJo.

"And the blankets and
swings," said Pedro.

"Uh-oh!" said Katie

Woo. "I think I have been

a meanie."

"For sure!" said Pedro

and JoJo.

"I'm sorry!" said Katie. "I won't be a meanie anymore. Is it okay if I share the sea with you?"

"Yes!" said her friends.

And there were plenty of waves for everyone!

About the Author

Fran Manushkin is the author of many popular picture books, including *How Mama Brought the Spring; Baby, Come Out!; Latkes and Applesauce: A Hanukkah Story;* and *The Tushy Book.* There is a real Katie Woo — she's Fran's great-niece — but she never gets in half the trouble of the Katie Woo in the books. Fran writes on her beloved Mac computer in New York City, without the help of her two naughty cats, Cookie and Goldy.

About the Illustrator

Tammie Lyon began her love for drawing at a young age while sitting at the kitchen table with her dad. She continued her love of art and eventually attended the Columbus College of Art and Design, where she earned a bachelors degree in fine art. After a brief career as a professional ballet dancer, she decided to devote herself full time to illustration. Today she lives with her husband, Lee, in Cincinnati, Ohio. Her dogs, Gus and Dudley, keep her company as she works in her studio.

🏖 Glossary 🏖

castle (KASS-uhl)—a large building, often surrounded by a wall and a moat

driftwood (DRIFT-wud)—wood that floats ashore or is floating on water

empty (EMP-tee)—nothing inside

hungry (HUHNG-gree)—wanting food

insisted (in-SIST-id)—demanded very strongly

itchy (ICH-ee)—something that makes you want to scratch your skin

selfish (SEL-fish)—someone who is selfish puts his or her own feelings first and does not think of others

Discussion Questions

1. Have you ever been bossed around? How did it make you feel?

2. Katie, JoJo, and Pedro's day was almost ruined because they argued. Have you ever argued with a friend? How did you make up?

3. Everyone wishes that they could be the boss sometimes. What or who do you wish you could be the boss of?

Writing Prompts

1. Make a list of all the ways Katie was selfish.

2. Make a list of words that describe a good boss.

3. The boss of your school is the principal. Draw a picture of your principal. Write a sentence that describes what kind of boss he or she is.

Having Fun with Katie Woo

In *Boss of the World*, Katie Woo and her friends spend the day at the beach. Here is a fun game you can play the next time you go to the beach.

Spot It at the Beach

This game asks you to find items that can be seen at the beach. It is like a scavenger hunt, but you do not need to collect the items. Just check the item off your list.

What you need (one for each player):

- a pen
- a piece of paper

What you do:

1. Together, the players make a list of ten or more items to search for. For an extra challenge, make them as detailed as possible. Here are some examples:

   - a striped bathing suit
   - a beach ball of three or more colors
   - a towel with a superhero on it
   - a sailboat

2. When your list is done, start searching. Players should mark off the items as they spot them. They should also make a note of where they saw them. The first one to spot all the items on the list wins!